This
Treasure Cove Story
belongs to

_____

BIG HERO 6

A CENTUM BOOK 978-1-912396-79-5
Published in Great Britain by Centum Books Ltd.
This edition published 2018.

1 3 5 7 9 10 8 6 4 2

Centum Books Ltd, 20 Devon Square, Newton Abbot,
Devon, TQ12 2HR, UK.

www.centumbooksltd.co.uk | books@centumbooksltd.co.uk
CENTUM BOOKS Limited Reg. No. 07641486.

A CIP catalogue record for this book is available
from the British Library.

Printed in China.

centum

BIG HERO 6

A Treasure Cove Story

Written by
Laura Hitchcock

Illustrated by
Victoria Ying
Mike Yamada

Designed by
Alfred Giuliani

HIRO and TADASHI

were brothers.

They **LOVED** to create fantastic new **INVENTIONS**!

Tadashi invented a **NURSE BOT** named Baymax. A special nursing chip inside Baymax allowed him to help sick people.

Hiro invented tiny machines called **MICROBOTS**.

Working together, the little microbots could create much larger objects! **Professor Callaghan**, a robotics teacher, was impressed.

After an accident at school, Hiro was
left without his brother. He felt all alone.

But Hiro was **not** alone. He had
Tadashi's nurse bot, *BAYMAX*!

Hiro and Baymax discovered that a villain named **YOKAI** had *stolen the microbots*!

Yokai sent a swarm of microbots to attack them.

Hiro's friends wanted to help...

...but **YOKAI** chased them! Hiro and his friends barely *ESCAPED* with their lives!

The team needed a plan to fight
Yokai. Hiro invented **high-tech
super suits for each of them!**

The suits gave everyone
superpowers!
Even Baymax got a new
suit – with *wings* and
a *rocket fist*!

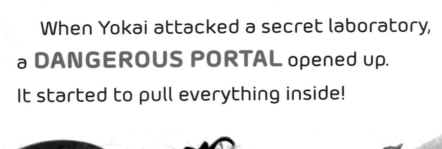

When Yokai attacked a secret laboratory,
a **DANGEROUS PORTAL** opened up.
It started to pull everything inside!

Then Hiro discovered that Yokai was

PROFESSOR CALLAGHAN!

Callaghan's daughter, Abigail, had been
lost when she entered the portal on a risky
mission. He wanted **REVENGE** on the
scientist who was responsible.

Baymax's sensors were
picking up **signs of life**.

HIRO and **BAYMAX** bravely flew into the portal.

They would **RESCUE** Abigail!

Hiro and Baymax found Abigail's lost space pod. But Baymax was damaged and running out of **POWER** fast!

Baymax had a **plan** to get them home.

Hiro hugged

his friend

goodbye.

Then Baymax used the last of his power to **blast his fist** out of the portal, taking Hiro and Abigail with it.

Hiro and Abigail were **SAFE!**
But Baymax
was gone.

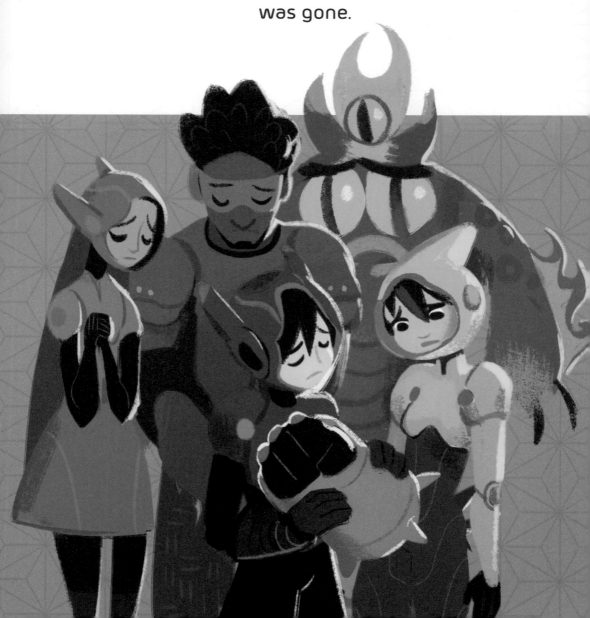

Even though Hiro had lost Baymax, he still
had the robot's *NURSING CHIP*.
That gave him an **idea**!

Treasure Cove Stories

•Book list may be subject to change.